PRAISE FOR M. L. BUCHMAN

Tom Clancy fans open to a strong female lead will clamor for more.

— *DRONE*, PUBLISHERS WEEKLY

Superb! Miranda is utterly compelling!

— *BOOKLIST,* STARRED REVIEW

Miranda Chase continues to astound and charm.

— BARB M.

Escape Rating: A. Five Stars! OMG just start with *Drone* and be prepared for a fantastic binge-read!

— READING REALITY

The best military thriller I've read in a very long time. Love the female characters.

— *DRONE,* SHELDON MCARTHUR, FOUNDER OF THE MYSTERY BOOKSTORE, LA

A fabulous soaring thriller.

— *Take Over at Midnight,* Midwest Book Review

Meticulously researched, hard-hitting, and suspenseful.

— *Pure Heat,* Publishers Weekly, starred review

Expert technical details abound, as do realistic military missions with superb imagery that will have readers feeling as if they are right there in the midst and on the edges of their seats.

— *Light Up the Night,* RT Reviews, 4 1/2 stars

Buchman has catapulted his way to the top tier of my favorite authors.

— Fresh Fiction

Nonstop action that will keep readers on the edge of their seats.

— *Take Over at Midnight,* Library Journal

M L. Buchman's ability to keep the reader right in the middle of the action is amazing.

— Long and Short Reviews

The only thing you'll ask yourself is, "When does the next one come out?"

— *Wait Until Midnight,* RT Reviews, 4 stars

The first...of (a) stellar, long-running (military) romantic suspense series.

— *The Night is Mine,* Booklist, "The 20 Best Romantic Suspense Novels: Modern Masterpieces"

I knew the books would be good, but I didn't realize how good.

— Night Stalkers series, Kirkus Reviews

Buchman mixes adrenalin-spiking battles and brusque military jargon with a sensitive approach.

— Publishers Weekly

13 times "Top Pick of the Month"

— Night Owl Reviews

TILL THE CLOWN SINGS

A FINAL CURTAIN COZY MYSTERY

M. L. BUCHMAN

All titles were previously published separately by Buchman Bookworks, Inc. All introductions are new to this collection.

Receive a free book and discover more by this author at: www.mlbuchman.com

Cover images:

Actors in baroque costumes © paseven

SIGN UP FOR M. L. BUCHMAN'S NEWSLETTER TODAY

and receive:

Release News

Free Short Stories

a Free Book

Get your free book today. Do it now.

free-book.mlbuchman.com

Other works by M. L. Buchman: *(* - also in audio)*

Action-Adventure Thrillers

Dead Chef

One Chef!
Two Chef!

Miranda Chase

*Drone**
*Thunderbolt**
*Condor**
*Ghostrider**
*Raider**
*Chinook**
*Havoc**
*White Top**

Romantic Suspense

Delta Force

*Target Engaged**
*Heart Strike**
*Wild Justice**
*Midnight Trust**

Firehawks

MAIN FLIGHT

Pure Heat
Full Blaze
*Hot Point**
*Flash of Fire**
Wild Fire

SMOKEJUMPERS

*Wildfire at Dawn**
*Wildfire at Larch Creek**
*Wildfire on the Skagit**

The Night Stalkers

MAIN FLIGHT

The Night Is Mine
I Own the Dawn
Wait Until Dark
Take Over at Midnight
Light Up the Night
Bring On the Dusk
By Break of Day

AND THE NAVY

Christmas at Steel Beach
Christmas at Peleliu Cove

WHITE HOUSE HOLIDAY

*Daniel's Christmas**
*Frank's Independence Day**
*Peter's Christmas**
*Zachary's Christmas**
*Roy's Independence Day**
*Damien's Christmas**

5E

Target of the Heart
Target Lock on Love
Target of Mine
Target of One's Own

Shadow Force: Psi

*At the Slightest Sound**
*At the Quietest Word**
*At the Merest Glance**
*At the Clearest Sensation**

White House Protection Force

*Off the Leash**
*On Your Mark**
*In the Weeds**

Contemporary Romance

Eagle Cove

Return to Eagle Cove
Recipe for Eagle Cove
Longing for Eagle Cove
Keepsake for Eagle Cove

Henderson's Ranch

*Nathan's Big Sky**
*Big Sky, Loyal Heart**
*Big Sky Dog Whisperer**

Other works by M. L. Buchman:

Contemporary Romance (cont)

Love Abroad

Heart of the Cotswolds: England
Path of Love: Cinque Terre, Italy

Where Dreams

Where Dreams are Born
Where Dreams Reside
*Where Dreams Are of Christmas**
Where Dreams Unfold
Where Dreams Are Written

Science Fiction / Fantasy

Deities Anonymous

Cookbook from Hell: Reheated
Saviors 101

Single Titles

The Nara Reaction
Monk's Maze
the Me and Elsie Chronicles

Non-Fiction

Strategies for Success

Managing Your Inner Artist/Writer
*Estate Planning for Authors**
Character Voice
*Narrate and Record Your Own Audiobook**

Short Story Series by M. L. Buchman:

Romantic Suspense

Delta Force

Th Delta Force Shooters
The Delta Force Warriors

Firehawks

The Firehawks Lookouts
The Firehawks Hotshots
The Firebirds

The Night Stalkers

The Night Stalkers 5D Stories
The Night Stalkers 5E Stories
The Night Stalkers CSAR
The Night Stalkers Wedding Stories

US Coast Guard

White House Protection Force

Contemporary Romance

Eagle Cove

Henderson's Ranch*

Where Dreams

Action-Adventure Thrillers

Dead Chef

Miranda Chase Origin Stories

Science Fiction / Fantasy

Deities Anonymous

Other

The Future Night Stalkers
Single Titles

ABOUT THIS TITLE

The Opera's Diva Is Dead! **Before** ***the fat lady sang.***

Assistant Stage Manager Jenny Caruthers *survived the opera cast's egos for four weeks of rehearsals, only to have the nightmare diva miss the final rehearsal curtain call. Why? She's dead on the backstage floor. Very annoying.*

Did the fat lady die on Jenny's watch from a heart attack, general nastiness, or was there more to the scene than hit the stage? She doesn't lack for suspects.

The diva's moody tenor husband? The soprano who envied the diva's fame? The well-built baritone with nefarious plans of his own?

Jenny must unravel the mystery before the clown sings and the final curtain falls.

1

JENNY CARUTHERS HAD THOUGHT MORE THAN ONCE about killing the diva Frau Helga Dempsey over the four weeks of rehearsal. It would make her life much easier, but murdering the lead soprano would truly screw up the production. *Pagliacci* was opening at Seattle's Emerald City Opera tomorrow night, and the show must go on.

But now Jenny had an even bigger mess on her hands than herding a couple dozen opera-sized egos around Seattle.

For four weeks she'd seen to everyone's demands no matter how ridiculous. That was her job as the assistant stage manager in charge of the cast.

Chester Dempsey, the diva's husband, couldn't sing unless a glass of fresh-squeezed, room-temperature lemon juice was close to hand along with a spittoon so that he could gargle with it to clear his throat just before he stepped onstage. High strung and annoying like most tenors were, he spent more time worrying and fussing than actually onstage and singing. And now her hands were not only wrinkled, they would forever smell like furniture polish.

Vicki Malone, the lead of the village chorus, and chief understudy to the diva was among the easiest of the lot. As long as she had the Wrestling Channel streaming to her hotel room twenty-four hours a day—it was in her contract—she complained very little.

Trevor Jackson, like so many baritones, was the villain onstage but a surprisingly pleasant man offstage. His easygoing manner had won the surprised appreciation of the entire backstage crew. The challenge the costume department had to overcome in fitting his *form* into a tight pair of pants had certainly won those ladies' appreciation and many speculative whispers, which Jenny did her best to ignore.

After all, Jenny had found herself a beau with two huge advantages, in addition to being a great guy. First, Max's schedule as a Seattle Police detective was at least as nuts as hers working at the opera, so they had a no-fault last-second-changes-are-fine agreement. Crisis calls in mid-date were accepted on either side with a shrug and a quick kiss. Second, he had absolutely nothing to do with the Emerald City Opera or even the theater, which was such a huge bonus she could barely stand it.

For not killing the ultimate worst member of the

cast, the diva Frau Helga Dempsey, Jenny had been granted two good things and one bad one.

First, she hadn't gone to jail for murder. It would probably put a serious crimp in her relationship with Max to be limited to conjugal visits.

Second, the diva had almost been tolerable to her this week, after four weeks of true hell.

Third, the bad one—which was really pissing her off—someone else had done in the diva the night before opening without even inviting her to participate.

Now there was a dead soprano on her stage!

2

IN THE FINAL DRESS REHEARSAL, THE MASSIVE WOMAN had done her *de rigueur* soprano fat-lady song. Then, per the script, been stabbed onstage by her betrayed-tenor husband.

Actually *Pagliacci* was a play within a play. Chester Dempsey was playing the actor Canio who was performing as the clown Pagliaccio in a play within the opera's story itself.

As if that wasn't confusing enough.

So, his wife in real life (the diva from the lowest levels of Dante's *Inferno*), was also his wife in the opera (the fair Nedda), who was also his wife in the stage play, Colombina. It would have been fine if the diva hadn't insisted on being called by the correct name *to assist her in maintaining the necessary verisimilitudes of characterization despite the impinging reality.*

The challenge was telling when she was actually

acting and which role, or often *roles*, she was playing at any one time. Was she Colombina, Nedda posing as Colombina, or the terribly annoying Frau Helga *being* the Diva.

The other crew members teased Jenny about being a diva-savant, because even Director Kane wasn't right as often as Jenny managed. Bets were taken, she pocketed good bar money by betting on herself.

But, the curtain had come down on the dress rehearsal, and the diva was nowhere to be found for the post-performance curtain call. A gap of little more than thirty seconds and Frau Helga Dempsey had gone missing. Even for the whimsical soprano, this was quite surprising. The one thing she wasn't whimsical about was receiving her fair portion and more of the adulation.

So, after the heavy red drape had dropped for the last time, cutting off the awkward applause of the rehearsal audience, Director Kane had sent Jenny to track down the diva and find out what was wrong this time.

She'd pulled her long blond hair through the hole in the back of her Emerald City Opera ball cap and set out upon her quest.

Jenny had no success at first. She'd checked the catered backstage buffet. Nothing. The green room where ego-stroking fans were sometimes planted. Empty. The diva wasn't even issuing demands from her dressing room like the mad captain from the *The Flying Dutchman,* pacing his quarterdeck for eternity.

It was only as Jenny was going about the backstage areas to gather the partially drunk-and-gargled lemon juice glasses from the various places they'd been hidden, that Jenny discovered what had gone wrong.

What was wrong was where the last and mostly empty glass of lemon juice was kept in a dark corner behind the wagon used as a stage by the troupe of players within the opera's plot.

Right there, hidden in the shadows, as large as, well, an opera singer, the diva was lying dead.

Flat on her back: no blood, no knife wound, and no pulse.

3

JENNY SPEED-DIALED HER BOYFRIEND MAX BY INSTINCT. He arrived so fast that she knew he'd been hanging about outside the loading dock hoping to take her out for a late-night dinner and early-morning sex.

He called in the medical team and finally the coroner, who had declared it a probable heart attack, pending autopsy.

Chester Dempsey, clearly deep in his role as fussy tenor-husband, suggested that really wasn't necessary, but Director Kane had pulled him aside and convinced him that they had to be sure.

Trevor, the baritone of the famous endowment, who had been so little trouble these last weeks, stepped up to the mark and became Chester's comforter for the evening. Which meant he took him out with the stated plan to get good and drunk together.

Jenny and Max's late-night dinner had turned into a sandwich from the stage-left buffet, kept well stocked as mandated in the dead diva's contract. Early-morning sex had been abandoned in exchange for a dozen meetings and much rapid phone work. And in trying not to watch in horror as four particularly robust stagehands were needed to assist the two ambulance drivers struggling to lift the dead diva onto a stretcher.

Vicki Malone had, unusually for a soprano, actually prepared for the understudy role. No problem there. She even knew most of the stage blocking and moved about the stage with a smooth agility—she was only about a quarter of the diva's size—into the proper places with only minimal hints from the other singers.

To replace her previous role as the lead soprano of the villager *audience,* had taken some quick negotiations with the New York agent of a local Seattle artist. The emergency would ultimately pay her triple what she'd have gotten if she'd landed the role in the first place.

During the quickly arranged afternoon rehearsal, Vicki and an only slightly hung-over Chester went through their paces without a hitch.

Their Canio and Nedda sparked and flared, fiery energy between them fueled brilliant arias.

Their roles for the play within the opera, Pagliaccio and Colombina, wooed and fought and sang—and ultimately stabbed. What Vicki's voice lacked in the sheer power commanded by the diva was counter-balanced by her smoother, gentler nuances on the vocal flourishes.

The Emerald City Opera had a hit on their hands.

4

MAX CAME AROUND AFTER THE REHEARSAL BUT BEFORE everyone left for dinner. He began the interviews. Those went so fast that Jenny and Max were at McMenamin's bar across from the opera house with plenty of time for dinner before the first-call to the stage.

They found a quiet booth toward the back. The tall-backed dark wood benches, generous cushions, and dim lighting was half Seattle bistro and half collapsing Scottish pub. It felt like a cozy date even if it wasn't only four hours to an opening night curtain.

"What do you know?" Jenny ordered a steamed-clams appetizer and a mushroom-Swiss burger with fries. Max ordered spaghetti and meatballs, a pint of Guinness, and helped her with the clams when they arrived. She hadn't slept in over thirty-six hours, which was about normal for an opening, let alone a diva replacement. So she opted for a strawberry lemonade instead of a beer. Her body had already stopped reacting to caffeine, so she'd give sugar a try.

"Not much, I'm afraid." Max started a game of footsie under the table.

One of many reasons why Jenny liked him.

"Heart failure, which shouldn't be a surprise. We didn't think anything much of it until the coroner's autopsy."

That was another reason why they were so compatible. He could discuss anything about a case over a meal and she didn't lose her appetite. She'd seen too many staged, tragic, sung-at-length deaths to be shocked by any of the merely gruesome details of a real one.

"What did the coroner find?" She piled the lettuce, tomato, and red onion onto her burger and bit in. Her moan of near-ecstasy elicited that great baritone laugh that Max brought along as part of the package.

He cut into a meatball.

"The lividity is greater than would be expected from a simple collapse or fall. Especially based on the known time of death."

"Lividity?"

He stole a French fry, she kicked him under the table. Not too hard.

"When you die, the blood settles to the lowest point. She had more lividity than normal, as if she'd fallen from a height of seven to ten feet. At least the coroner thinks so, if she'd been a normal-sized woman. He's less sure about a woman built on the diva's scale. The only problem is, there's nothing that high anywhere near the body site."

She took a swallow of his beer. In fair exchange, Jenny didn't kick him when he took the next French fry.

"I talked to the rest of the cast and crew, but no one saw or heard anything unusual. It's now officially just a heart attack. We'll hold the file open for a day or so, but I don't expect any change."

The conversation turned to more pleasant topics, like their plans for a weekend hike with camping and making love out-of-doors as soon as this opera was over.

Jenny felt cheated.

If a diva was going to die, it should have been something more fittingly tragic than falling over dead of a heart attack. Colombina, the costume the diva had been wearing when she died, wasn't supposed to simply fall over dead either. She was supposed to die stabbed to death by her dressed-like-a-clown jealous-tenor husband as she cried out to her villager-attired baritone lover.

As she'd died in costume, Jenny half wondered if they'd bury her as Helga Dempsy or Colombina.

5

THE OPENING NIGHT PERFORMANCE WAS ATTENDED AS only an opera in Seattle would be. Patrons arrived garbed in tuxedos and evening gowns, and sat beside the truly wealthy garbed in jeans and a Microsoft hoodie. Even an opening night at the opera did not gainsay a Seattleite's sense of entitlement to a complete lack of style.

Backstage, the mayhem was only a little worse than usual.

Jenny checked in with Chester Dempsey in his dressing room first, letting him know his glasses of lemon juice were in place.

"Thank you. I'm fine, dear. Thank you so much for your concern. Helga and I had over twenty good years since we did *Tannhäuser* together at the Staatsoper in Dresden." The way that all opera singers measured time, by the performance. "She was too young to pass on, but she'd have been the first to insist that the show must go on."

Jenny knew from four weeks of painful personal experience that the dear departed diva would have been the first to insist that someone call an ambulance at three minutes to curtain if she'd had so much as a hangnail. Maybe Chester wished to remember his wife as she'd once, perhaps, been.

Vicki Malone had appeared to be floating about her dressing room when Jenny arrived.

As, Jenny supposed, Vicki should be.

If she sang as well as she had this afternoon, she would make international news for so successfully stepping into an important role on such short notice. Emerald City was the fifth largest opera company in the States now and had a substantial reputation that could truly boost a singer's career.

Several costume mistresses were in attendance on Vicki, still putting the finishing touches on her drastically more slender costume. The usual jokes about handsome Trevor's suitability as her lover Silvio tittered back and forth.

When they asked Vicki if she knew of the scale of Trevor's other endowments, Jenny headed for the hall. As she closed the door she heard Vicki laugh brightly, "So the diva told me."

Jenny continued her rounds, spending extra time with the new lead soprano of the villagers to make sure she was settled in. Thankfully she and Vicki were of similar scale, so the alterations to that costume had been quickly achieved.

At a hurried meeting with Val, the stage manager, and the other three assistant stage managers, they all agreed they were as ready as usual for an opening night. Which meant any train wrecks were likely to be mere derailments.

The performance went impeccably.

Everyone got to places on time with only a minimum of prodding. The singing was so dynamic that the cast when off-stage didn't wander far, rather they all stood together in the wings and listened.

Chester-Canio roared in true anguish when he discovered Vicki-Nedda had a lover. He cried in triumph when he almost caught presumptuous Trevor-villager. He wept through "Vesti la Giubba" as he clothed himself as Pagliaccio the Clown at the bottom of Act I.

In Act II the mockery of Chester-Canio-Pagliaccio continued over his cheating wife Vicki-Nedda-Colombina.

Jenny was rocked to her heart at Chester's desperate cry of pain upon discovering the betrayal of Vicki's love for Trevor-villager-baritone. Pagliaccio's final anguish, when he has killed his wife and her lover then turns to the audience, created a silence so complete that no one even breathed in the sweeping three-thousand seat house.

"La commedia è finita!" Pagliaccio the Clown sang *the*

play is over in a final cry of such perfect pain that the crowd roared to their feet. Whatever else the man's shortcomings, Chester's voice and pacing were superb.

No question, they'd be sold out when the reviews hit the streets and the box office opened tomorrow. The half-filled houses in the mid-week performances would be history.

Even as the curtain came down and rose again to the ongoing standing ovation, Jenny began collecting the glasses of lemon juice.

She peeked behind the player's wagon last of all but there was no dead body this time. She poured the full glass into the spittoon to make it easier to carry off to the wash-up sink.

Jenny had been awake for two long days and one longer night. Even if Max's text hadn't said he was out on a call, all she'd be able to do tonight was stumble to her bed and sleep.

6

THE OPERA'S TRIUMPH CONTINUED THROUGH THREE more nights. The fourth night something was off and by the fifth, even the audience appeared to sense it.

Jenny stopped Jimmy, one of the other assistant stage managers, on his way up to the sound booth. The radio simulcast was tonight and someone had to keep touch with the recording engineer.

"Did last night seem off to you?"

He shrugged. He didn't have much of an ear but was a good technician. That's why he'd been assigned to assist with the sound and light crews. There were times Jenny envied him the role, but at least working with the cast was never dull.

Something was definitely off.

Jenny just couldn't put her finger on it.

She went backstage and slipped up to the stage manager's station, close beside the stage-left edge of the stage. Val was a very serious Jewish guy. Any guy named Valentine by their parents was bound to grow up with no sense of humor. He barely came up to Jenny's shoulder. His job was to coordinate every activity in the theater during the performance. She didn't have to ask, they traded a look and both went back to work—Val heard it too.

Jenny prayed it wasn't a cursed show. She had a date with Max tonight and there was only this performance and then closing night tomorrow before the opera came down. They needed just two good nights and she'd be done with the whole lot of them.

But it had been too good to last.

Chester was definitely off tonight. Real anger thickened his tone, roughening his normally world-class voice.

Vicki Malone's *I will always be yours!* to the handsome Trevor sounded overly dramatic, even for the role of Colombina.

By a form of magic that Jenny hoped to learn someday, Val held the performance together, perhaps through sheer will. Afterward, everyone retreated to their respective corners and prayed for one last show—good or otherwise, as long as it was over without any more corpses.

7

It was while Jenny was in the darkest corner of the set, again behind the player's wagon, emptying the glass of fresh-squeezed lemon juice, that she heard them.

Somewhere nearby, among the overlapping curtains, a couple were making exactly the sounds she hoped to be making later with Max. This was common enough around the theater that she did little more than wish the couple fun as she headed for the wash-up sink, and then the back door to head out.

She met Max at their back booth in McMenamin's. They decided to split a beer and an order of fried mushrooms before heading to her place.

"There's a chap with a head of steam on," Max observed, irony thick in his voice as they were debating whether an appetizer was enough or should they have dinner. Max knew from experience the state of Jenny's refrigerator during a production.

Jenny leaned out of the booth to see who had caught his attention.

Chester Dempsey barreled up to the long main bar and slapped down a bill. "Crown Royal XR, and keep it coming."

Jenny had two thoughts.

One, they paid opera singers way too much—eXtra Rare meant being eXtremely Rich to drink it.

Two, they had to get out of here fast and she had to turn off her phone if she wanted to keep her plans with Max.

She followed her own advice. Phones silenced and heads down, they escaped fast.

8

After doing their own bit of somewhat more private moaning, Jenny lay in Max's arms while he slept. He'd be on duty in four hours, so she didn't begrudge him the luxury of sleep after sex, another part of their no-fault pact.

As she lay there, mellow right down to her toes but wide awake, she began to wonder just who had been among those curtains backstage after the performance.

The groan had a familiar sound. Not a mighty groan as one might expect from a large woman, but a smoother, more graceful sound.

Vicki Malone. And who had caused the fair Colombina to make such a sound after being stabbed by her husband?

Clearly not Chester Dempsey, soothing himself in a bar with thirty-dollar-a-shot whisky. And yet, now that she thought of it, that was who she'd expected. As a matter of fact, it had almost been a certainty they'd been lovers. If not before the diva died, then certainly within hours afterward.

For the last week, the two of them had caused her so little trouble, and made so few demands, Jenny had thought that pair might, just might turn into actual human beings. Even Trevor's rare requests were more than she had heard from Chester and Vicki after the death of the diva.

And their performance onstage had cast sparks that were impossible to miss.

Until the last two performances.

Jenny slipped out of bed and went to the window of her one-bedroom apartment. In a peek-a-boo view between two taller buildings, it looked out over Seattle Center, down upon the Opera Hall. When she'd first moved in, it felt as if the shadowed Hall somehow always had its eye on her. Now, because she knew turnabout was fair play, she felt that the Opera Hall knew that she had her eye on it as well.

And if she could see through those brick walls?

Vicki Malone had made a sound that rose from a woman when a man, the right man...

Jenny's gaze shifted and she could see her own smile reflected by the darkened window.

Trevor the notoriously-endowed baritone could certainly cause Vicki Malone to make that sound.

Jenny grabbed a robe and belted it on as she

slipped into the living room and closed the door on the sleeping Max.

She set to pacing by the soft lights of Seattle glowing beyond her living room window. She circled from the dark television screen, around the white thrift-store sofa, on which most of her and Max's clothes had been abandoned, over to the efficient little kitchen, and once more around the far end of the sofa. The small black coffee table that also served as her dining table completed the circuit.

There was more going on. She merely needed to set the right scene.

Chester Dempsey had come to the bar in a rage, perhaps after discovering Vicki and Trevor together. Chester, despite his magnificent tenor, had always struck her as a bit effete, too delicate of manner for drastic deeds, so Jenny doubted that he had confronted the lovers—instead personally making the bartender's night.

She went into the kitchen to pour herself a glass of orange juice.

The glass was nearly full when the picture formed fully in her head. She knew exactly what she'd been missing.

Jenny turned on her television, leaving the sound off, and began flipping channels.

9

When Max left at some obscenely indecent hour, definitely before noon, Jenny managed to mumble at him.

"Did you close the file on the diva yet?"

"Not yet. Been busy."

She nodded her head, on her way back to sleep. "Don't. And come to the show tonight."

10

JENNY WENT TO THE THEATER EARLY AND TOOK A flashlight with her. What had been hidden back in the dark corner of the set, now came to light.

Max showed up at the bottom of the first act.

Jenny kissed him behind a black leg of drapery which hung down to mask stage right. Then she whispered in his ear.

"Did you bring handcuffs?"

"Flexicuffs." The long plastic strips, that once tightened around the wrists could only be removed by cutting. "Why, have you got ideas?" His whisper tickled her cheek.

"Why Detective Max Wellton. I am shocked. I'm a good girl I am." She gave it her best Eliza Doolittle Cockney. Though it gave her some ideas as well. Max would look great in them.

She waited until Act I ended and the singers had

all moved to their dressing rooms for the intermission. Then she led Max behind the player's wagon.

"Exhibit A." She shone her flashlight on a bit of black lace underwear lying tangled against the bottom of a black drape. "This is where Vicki Malone and Trevor Jackson had a tryst last night."

"That gives *me* an idea or two."

She shifted her flashlight across the floor before he could act on any of them.

"Exhibit B. This is where the Diva lay."

That sobered Max up enough to eye her carefully and then nod for her to continue.

"Exhibit C." She felt like one of those TV courtroom dramas. "Notice the clean spot on the stage's plank flooring? Not by her feet where you'd expect it if perhaps she had slipped on something wet, but by her head. Far enough away that we didn't notice it."

"As if the diva had slipped in it then tumbled head over heels." Max eyed the area then shook his head. "But she doesn't strike me as the somersault sort. So what did she trip on?"

Now Jenny directed her flashlight onto the glass of fresh-squeezed lemon juice. "I told you about Chester's need for these, for his throat."

Max nodded.

"This one is odd because it's not near any stage entrance. And it has been full every single night except one. The night the diva died, it was almost empty. If you kneel down and smell that spot on the floor, it is quite lemony."

Max did so, then nodded his agreement. He looked up at her from where he knelt and she couldn't help running her fingers through his thick dark hair for a moment.

"But if she slipped on the slick floor here, how did she flip end for end? I can't see Chester shifting a woman of the diva's heft."

"That's cheating, Detective Max Wellton. You're trying to jump to the end of the scene. First we need to get each of the characters of this little drama into their pre-curtain positions in order to see the beauty of it."

Jenny had to admit that it was well planned.

"Our first player, the diva, was trying to force the second player, the handsome Trevor, to become her lover and he wasn't happy about it. She was probably promising him better roles in future productions, or no decent roles ever again if he refused."

"How do you know?" Max climbed to his feet and pulled out a pad to start taking notes.

She could hear the crew-hands shifting the set in preparation for Act II. She still had ten minutes.

"Vicki mentioned that the diva had told her of Trevor's affliction."

"Affliction?"

"Apparently he's built like a horse."

"Oh." Max actually stopped taking notes and hesitated.

Jenny kissed him. "You have no worries in that department, lover."

He looked down to hide his relief.

Men were so cute.

"Anyway, Trevor wasn't happy about the diva's demands."

"And you know this..."

"By how cheerful he became after her death. He abruptly became Chester's best friend. Chester and Vicki were in cahoots for exact opposite reasons. Chester was very pleased to replace one soprano in his bed with another, which I expect he had been doing for some time, and Vicki was thrilled to trade up in the world. With the diva out of the way, she also made her mark in the press. Then last night, her exceptional reviews giving her the confidence that she could make her success even without Chester's aid, she dumped him in favor of the handsome-and-hung Trevor."

"This is more confusing than one of your operas." She'd tried explaining some of the convoluted opera plots and he'd insisted that even psychotic murderers were simpler to understand.

"You saw it yourself at the bar last night. It left Chester completely furious. Just like in the opera, the clown being played for a fool after the death of his cheating wife. It made him a cuckold in every direction: he with Vicki, the diva's attempts with Trevor, and then Vicki hitting the jackpot with Trevor."

Max grunted an agreement. "So who did it?"

"Did what?"

"Killed the diva."

"They all did, Max." She brushed her hand across his cheek. "It was a truly operatic moment."

He still wasn't seeing it.

"Trevor," she imitated one person leading another, "must have led the diva to this dark spot at the close of the Second Act. She would follow, despite missing a curtain call—it was only a dress rehearsal after all—thinking that she had triumphed and was finally headed for exactly the sort of tryst that Vicki and Trevor had last night."

Jenny shifted, lifted the full glass of lemon juice as if to pour it onto the floor. But she didn't want to clean it up, so she set the glass back by the empty spittoon.

"Chester made the floor slick by dumping his whole glass juice in a very specific position close behind..."

"Vicki?" Max was scratching his head. "She's the only one left, but that makes no sense. What could she do against a woman several times her size?"

"This." She maneuvered Max until he stood where the diva must have stood, unsteady in the middle of the slick wetness of spilled lemon juice. Max was at least six inches taller than Jenny, and fifty pounds heavier, which looked great on him as it was all cop muscle.

She grabbed Max by the collar with one hand and wrapped her arm around his neck. With a sharp twist and a sideways lean, she leveraged him over her hip and shoulder and slammed him down on the floor, easing his fall at the last second.

"Ow! What the hell, Jen?" He groaned as he lay there, flat on his back, exactly where the diva had lain.

"Wow!" Jenny had to remember that trick. "It actually worked."

She helped Max back to his feet. His ego was clearly shaken by the experience. She'd have kissed it to make it better but she was running out of time.

"Sorry, I didn't expect to pull that off. I found it on *Smackdown TV* last night. It's called a Rolling Snapmare. Vicki is a total addict of the Wrestling Channel. She'd definitely know that move, way better than me. She stood on this dry part of the floor while the diva stood where you were on the slippery part. Then Vicki flipped the diva so hard that it looked like a high fall, even with nowhere to fall from."

Max rubbed at his neck as if it was hurting for several reasons. She hurried to explain before he could cut her off.

"The shock was enough to induce the heart attack. Maybe they were counting on knocking her out so that they could suffocate her, but they got lucky. The woman died while the three of them rushed out front to take their bows without her."

Max rubbed his neck one last time, then went to retrieve his pad and pen where they'd shot out of his hands as Jenny flipped him head over heels.

"You did it, Jen. It all fits. I'll call a couple squad

cars and we'll arrest them. This is all conjecture, but I'm sure we can get at least one of them to talk and give up the other two."

Over the backstage monitors, Val called, "Three minutes to places, top of Act II."

"Max, honey. I'll promise to be especially good to you if you'll do me just one favor."

"What's that?"

"This is the last act on the opera's closing night." She kissed him long and slow then pulled back until they were just a breath apart.

"Why is that important?"

"Could you hold off the arrests until after Pagliacci's '*La commedia è finita!*'? The show's not over until the clown sings."

DRONE (EXCERPT)

IF YOU ENJOYED THAT, YOU'LL LOVE MIRANDA CHASE!

DRONE (EXCERPT)

Flight 630 at 37,000 feet
12 nautical miles north of
Santa Fe, New Mexico, USA

THE FLIGHT ATTENDANT STEPPED UP TO HER SEAT—4E—which had never been her favorite on a 767-300. At least the cabin setup was in the familiar 261-seat, 2-class configuration, currently running at a seventy-three percent load capacity with a standard crew of ten and one ride-along FAA inspector in the cockpit jump seat.

"Excuse me, are you Miranda Chase?"

She nodded.

The attendant made a face that she couldn't interpret.

A frown? Did that indicate anger?

He turned away before she could consider the possibilities and, without another word, returned to his station at the front of the cabin.

Miranda once again straightened the emergency exit plan that the flight's vibrations kept shifting askew in its pocket.

This flight from yesterday's meeting at LAX to today's DC lunch meeting at the National Transportation Safety Board's headquarters departed so early that she'd decided to spend the night in the airline's executive lounge working on various aviation accident reports. She never slept on a flight and would have to catch up on her sleep tonight.

Miranda felt the shift as the plane turned into a modest five-degree bank to the left. The bright rays of dawn over the New Mexico desert shifted from the left-hand windows to the right side.

At due north, she heard the Rolls-Royce RB211 engines (quite a pleasant high tone compared to the Pratt & Whitney PW4000 that she always found unnerving) ease off ever so slightly, signaling a slow descent. The pilot was transitioning from an eastbound course that would be flown at an odd number of thousands of feet to a westbound one that must be flown at an even number.

The flight attendant then picked up the intercom phone and a loud squawk sounded through the cabin. Most people would be asleep and there were soft complaints and rustling down the length of the aircraft.

"We regret to inform you that there is an emergency on the ground. I repeat, there is nothing wrong with the plane. We are being routed back to Las Vegas, where we will disembark one passenger, refuel, and then continue our flight to DC. Our apologies for the inconvenience."

There were now shouts of complaint all up and down the aisle.

The flight attendant was staring straight at her as he slammed the intercom back into its cradle with significantly greater force than was required to seat it properly.

Oh. It was her they would be disembarking. That meant there was a crash in need of an NTSB investigator—a major one if they were flying back an hour in the wrong direction.

Thankfully, she always had her site kit with her.

For some reason, her seatmate was muttering something foul. Miranda ignored it and began to prepare herself.

Only the crash mattered.

She straightened the exit plan once more. It had shifted the other way with the changing harmonic from the RB211 engines.

Chengdu, Central China

AIR FORCE MAJOR WANG FAN EASED BACK ON THE joystick of the final prototype Shenyang J-31 jet—designed exclusively for the People's Liberation Army Air Force. In response, China's newest fighter jet leapt upward like a catapult's missile from the PLAAF base in the flatlands surrounding the towering city of Chengdu.

It felt as he'd just been grasped by Chen Mei-Li. Never had a woman made him feel like such a man.

ABOUT THE AUTHOR

USA Today and Amazon #1 Bestseller M. L. "Matt" Buchman started writing on a flight south from Japan to ride his bicycle across the Australian Outback. Just part of a solo around-the-world trip that ultimately launched his writing career.

From the very beginning, his powerful female heroines insisted on putting character first, *then* a great adventure. He's since written over 60 action-adventure thrillers and military romantic suspense novels. And just for the fun of it: 100 short stories, and a fast-growing pile of read-by-author audiobooks.

Booklist says: "3X Top 10 of the Year." PW says: "Tom Clancy fans open to a strong female lead will clamor for more." His fans say: "I want more now...of everything." That his characters are even more insistent than his fans is a hoot.

As a 30-year project manager with a geophysics degree who has designed and built houses, flown and jumped out of planes, and solo-sailed a 50' ketch, he is awed by what is possible. More at: www.mlbuchman.com.

Other works by M. L. Buchman: *(* - also in audio)*

Action-Adventure Thrillers

Dead Chef

One Chef!
Two Chef!

Miranda Chase

*Drone**
*Thunderbolt**
*Condor**
*Ghostrider**
*Raider**
*Chinook**
*Havoc**
*White Top**

Romantic Suspense

Delta Force

*Target Engaged**
*Heart Strike**
*Wild Justice**
*Midnight Trust**

Firehawks

MAIN FLIGHT

Pure Heat
Full Blaze
*Hot Point**
*Flash of Fire**
Wild Fire

SMOKEJUMPERS

*Wildfire at Dawn**
*Wildfire at Larch Creek**
*Wildfire on the Skagit**

The Night Stalkers

MAIN FLIGHT

The Night Is Mine
I Own the Dawn
Wait Until Dark
Take Over at Midnight
Light Up the Night
Bring On the Dusk
By Break of Day

AND THE NAVY

Christmas at Steel Beach
Christmas at Peleliu Cove

WHITE HOUSE HOLIDAY

*Daniel's Christmas**
*Frank's Independence Day**
*Peter's Christmas**
*Zachary's Christmas**
*Roy's Independence Day**
*Damien's Christmas**

5E

Target of the Heart
Target Lock on Love
Target of Mine
Target of One's Own

Shadow Force: Psi

*At the Slightest Sound**
*At the Quietest Word**
*At the Merest Glance**
*At the Clearest Sensation**

White House Protection Force

*Off the Leash**
*On Your Mark**
*In the Weeds**

Contemporary Romance

Eagle Cove

Return to Eagle Cove
Recipe for Eagle Cove
Longing for Eagle Cove
Keepsake for Eagle Cove

Henderson's Ranch

*Nathan's Big Sky**
*Big Sky, Loyal Heart**
*Big Sky Dog Whisperer**

Other works by M. L. Buchman:

Contemporary Romance (cont)

Love Abroad

Heart of the Cotswolds: England
Path of Love: Cinque Terre, Italy

Where Dreams

Where Dreams are Born
Where Dreams Reside
*Where Dreams Are of Christmas**
Where Dreams Unfold
Where Dreams Are Written

Science Fiction / Fantasy

Deities Anonymous

Cookbook from Hell: Reheated
Saviors 101

Single Titles

The Nara Reaction
Monk's Maze
the Me and Elsie Chronicles

Non-Fiction

Strategies for Success

Managing Your Inner Artist/Writer
*Estate Planning for Authors**
Character Voice
*Narrate and Record Your Own Audiobook**

Short Story Series by M. L. Buchman:

Romantic Suspense

Delta Force

Th Delta Force Shooters
The Delta Force Warriors

Firehawks

The Firehawks Lookouts
The Firehawks Hotshots
The Firebirds

The Night Stalkers

The Night Stalkers 5D Stories
The Night Stalkers 5E Stories
The Night Stalkers CSAR
The Night Stalkers Wedding Stories

US Coast Guard

White House Protection Force

Contemporary Romance

Eagle Cove

Henderson's Ranch*

Where Dreams

Action-Adventure Thrillers

Dead Chef

Miranda Chase Origin Stories

Science Fiction / Fantasy

Deities Anonymous

Other

The Future Night Stalkers
Single Titles

SIGN UP FOR M. L. BUCHMAN'S NEWSLETTER TODAY

and receive:

Release News

Free Short Stories

a Free Book

Get your free book today. Do it now.

free-book.mlbuchman.com

www.ingramcontent.com/pod-product-compliance
Lightning Source LLC
LaVergne TN
LVHW050944080826
845145LV00004B/1408